TREASURE TOWN

DOUG WILHELM

Illustrations by
SARAH-LEE TERRAT

This book is for Henry Woodard,
who started it

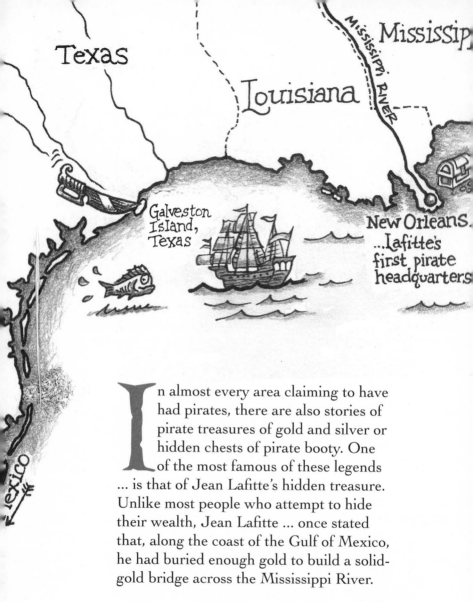

In almost every area claiming to have had pirates, there are also stories of pirate treasures of gold and silver or hidden chests of pirate booty. One of the most famous of these legends ... is that of Jean Lafitte's hidden treasure. Unlike most people who attempt to hide their wealth, Jean Lafitte ... once stated that, along the coast of the Gulf of Mexico, he had buried enough gold to build a solid-gold bridge across the Mississippi River.

from the book *Florida Pirates*
by James & Sarah Kaserman

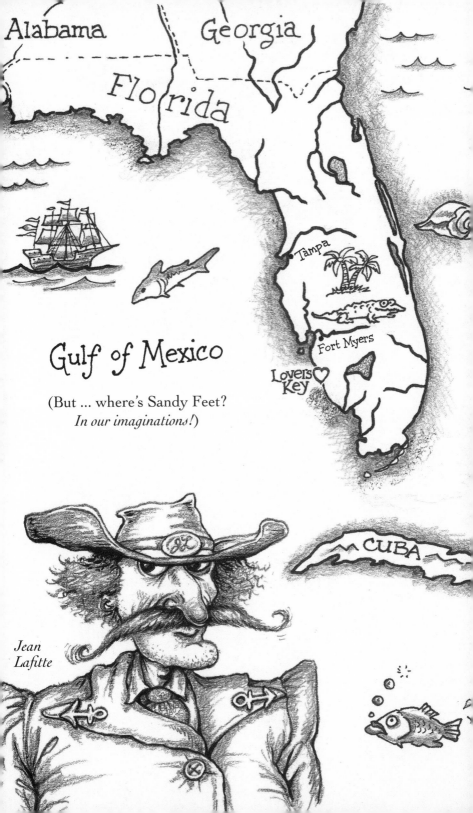

Alabama

Georgia

Florida

Gulf of Mexico

(But ... where's Sandy Feet?
In our imaginations!)

Tampa

Fort Myers

Lovers
Key

CUBA

Jean
Lafitte

WORDS TO KNOW IN TREASURE TOWN

Alaska. A state up north where people went to dig for gold.

Boxcar. In a freight train, the long boxlike thing that holds cargo. Usually, cargo.

Doubloon (say "dubloon"). A kind of gold coin that's in sunken ships and treasure chests. A doubloon would be worth a lot of money ... if you could find one.

Geyser. A flowing tower of water. Or other stuff.

Gulf of Mexico. A big huge body of water between Florida, Louisiana, Texas and Mexico. Once a haunt of pirates.

Intuition. When you get a feeling about something. You know?

Flabbergasted. Thunderstruck.

Thunderstruck. Flabbergasted.

Burr pickin', hang flangin', foul-smellin', fling blingin', fur flinginest, wing dinginest, sand flanginest ...
Never mind! Never mind! And now the story!

CHAPTER 1

THE PIRATE DINER

ONE AFTERNOON in Sandy Feet, Florida, three kids sat on stools inside the Pirate Diner. The kids' names were Luis, Hayley B. and Speedup. They came here every day after school, to hear an old story.

"Tell us *one* more time," whispered Hayley B.

Betty Jo-Ann the waitress set down three glasses of water on the counter. Some days the kids had a little money, to buy blueberry muffins. Today, like most days, they didn't.

Betty Jo-Ann leaned over the counter.

"A cruel pirate," she said in a low voice.

"Oh. *Very* cruel," agreed Hayley B., bouncing on her stool.
"In this town," said Luis.
"Right here in Sandy Feet," said Betty Jo-Ann.
"Come on," said Speedup. "Tell about the treasure!"
Betty Jo-Ann smiled.

"All right," she said — "I'll tell you one more time."

The kids leaned in closer, to listen. Behind Betty Jo-Ann, in the window to the kitchen, Big Thermal the cook leaned on his elbows. He was listening, too.

"The old legend," Betty Jo-Ann began, "says that somewhere in this town, some of the gold stolen by that old pirate king, Jean Lafitte ..." she took a deep breath ... "is buried."

"And *that's* why this is the Pirate Diner," said Hayley B.

"Yeah," said Speedup. "Yeah!"

"And no one ever found it," said Hayley B.

"That's right," Betty Jo-Ann said, and smiled again. "Now you three scoot! I'll have paying customers coming in soon."

The kids hopped down and started for the door. But Luis came back. He stood at the counter on tiptoes. Betty Jo-Ann leaned down to listen.

Luis said, "Don't you ... think it would be on the beach? I mean, being a pirate's treasure and all. I've been thinking that's where it *would* be."

"Well," said Betty Jo-Ann.

Now all three kids were back, listening.

"Here's what I think," Betty Jo-Ann said. "If that treasure's on the beach, it must be buried way down deep."

"Because no one *ever* found it," Hayley B. said again.

"If we found it," Luis said, "I'd order everything in this whole diner! I'd eat it, too."

"Let's go find it," Speedup said. "Let's go!"

"But ... I don't know," Luis said. "We're just kids."

"We can do it," said Speedup. "We can. Let's *go*!"

He shot out the door. Hayley B. hurried out next. Luis looked like he wanted to ask something more ... but then he went, too.

. . .

As she wiped the counter, Betty Jo-Ann hummed a song. Behind her, Big Thermal chewed on a toothpick.

"How come you said that about the beach?" he asked. "Nobody really knows where that old pirate put his stuff. If there ever was any stuff."

Out the window, Betty Jo-Ann could see the three kids bustling up the street.

"There *could* be," she said. "And it could be there."

Big Thermal chewed on his toothpick.

"I bet there never was any treasure," he said. "It's just an old story."

"Maybe," Betty Jo-Ann said — "but those kids don't have too much. They need something to dream on."

Chapter 2

A Nice Jelly Doughnut

T HAT SAME TIME, just up the street, Chief Gherkin was about to enjoy a nice jelly doughnut. It was cloudy and cool, this afternoon in Sandy Feet. That's how the police chief liked it.

No trouble.

It wasn't sunny, so the town
beach was empty. There would be no
traffic jam later, full of sandy people with
sunburns. Honking their horns.

The chief didn't like honking horns and traffic
jams. He was the only person in Sandy Feet who didn't like
sunny beach days at all.

This, now, was a great time for a strawberry jelly
doughnut. Just sit in the cool police car, enjoy his snack and
watch the old afternoon freight train roll into town.

The old train clacked, and
clanked, and slowed down for the
crossing on Snackbar Street. The
light flashed, the bell clanged, and
the train stopped.

Then the doughnut stopped
halfway to Chief Gherkin's mouth.
Because the door of one boxcar
slid open, and these two *weirdos*
tumbled out.

Chief Gherkin did not like the looks of this. At all. When the door of a freight car opens and two dusty, smelly-looking weirdos tumble out in the middle of your town, on a nice quiet afternoon ... if you're the police chief, you don't like that.

Not one little bit.

Besides. These were the two oddest-looking weirdos the chief had ever seen.

CHAPTER 3

SOMETHING TO DIG WITH

THE THREE KIDS hustled up Snackbar Street.

"We need something to dig with," said Luis.

"My grandpa has a shovel," said Hayley B.

"Let's go get it!" said Speedup.

But Luis slowed down. He shook his head.

"I *want* to find the treasure," he said. "I always think about finding it. But how can we find some pirate's treasure buried under that whole beach? I mean, three kids and one shovel. And a whole beach?"

Hayley B. sniffed the sea breeze.

"I will use my intuition," she said.

"What's that?"

"I ... think it's when you get a feeling about something," Hayley B. said. "It's very mysterious."

Luis said, "Do you have a feeling about this?"

Hayley B. looked around. She looked down.

"I'm not really sure," she said.

"But your grandpa does have a shovel," said Luis.

"Oh yes."

"Let's go get it!" said Speedup.

So they hurried up Snackbar Street, toward Hayley B.'s grandpa's garage.

CHAPTER 4

NOT EXACTLY ALASKA

WHEN THOSE TWO WEIRDOS tumbled out of the freight car onto Snackbar Street, they noticed it was warm. It was *too* warm.

Yuke Johnson looked around. He saw palm trees. He said, "This don't look like Alaska."

Yuke held a shovel in his hand. The shovel was large. Yuke was large.

"Aw ... this ain't right at all," said Yuke's buddy Bug Luck, looking around too. Bug was small and raggedy. He took off his hat and shook his head.

"I knew it was gettin' warmer in there," Bug said. "I just thought it was you."

"It don't feel like Alaska," Yuke said. He plucked at the long woolen underwear beneath his giant overalls. He really was warm.

"It don't *seem* like Alaska," he said.

"*It ain't hang flangin' Alaska!*" hollered Bug Luck. "We meant to sneak on a train goin' north, so we could dig for gold. Looks to me like we got on one goin' south instead. Of all the burr-pickin', foul-smellin' bad luck I ever had, this is the fur flinginest, wing dinginest *worst*!"

He flang his old sweaty hat on the ground, stamped on it and grumbled some more.

"We won't never dig up no gold now," Bug said. "How can we get rich in a place like this? Where *are* we, anyways?"

Yuke didn't know. He was worried. His buddy Bug was upset. They went the wrong way. He needed to do something.

So Yuke did the one thing he knew how to do. He did the one thing he did very, very well.

He started to dig.

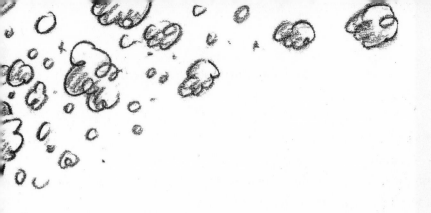

Yuke was big, and he could dig. He could dig stronger and faster and deeper than anyone else anywhere. *Anywhere.* That was how Bug Luck figured they would get rich for sure, digging for gold in Alaska.

But they weren't in Alaska. They were in Sandy Feet, Florida, and Yuke was digging right into Snackbar Street. He dug down through the street and kept on digging. Dirt flew up from his shovel like a geyser.

In his police car, Chief Gherkin dropped his doughnut. It made a strawberry smear in his lap, but the chief didn't notice. He was too flabbergasted at what he was seeing, right there on Snackbar Street.

He turned on the siren of his police car. He flicked on his whirling blue light.

"Dig up my town right in front of me — I don't *think* so," the chief said.

The police car came yowling down to where Yuke was digging. Yuke was down below the street, now — and just then he hit something hard. With a *chunk*.

Right as the police car came skidding up, Yuke, who was very strong, dug through the town's main water pipe.

A powerful geyser shot up fifteen feet in the air. On top of it was Chief Gherkin's police car. Inside the car, high up in the air, was a very wide-eyed chief.

Yuke Johnson looked up. Bug Luck looked up.

"Ho boy," said Bug. "We are in some trouble now."

. . .

On their way to Hayley B.'s grandpa's garage, Luis and Speedup and Hayley B. saw something weird. It was rising straight up from Snackbar Street. Like a geyser, with something on top.

"Whoa," said Luis.

"Let's go see what that is," said Speedup. "Let's go *see*!"

CHAPTER 5

A CROWD GATHERS

WELL, A CROWD GATHERED. In a small town like
Sandy Feet, if a police car gets stuck on top of a
water geyser, with the police chief *in* the car ... well,
a crowd will gather.

The whole town stood there. Nobody knew what to do.

"Somebody get me *down*," Chief Gherkin said from up
there.

"Why don't you sorta slide down, Chief?" said a skinny
guy who sold Ice Cream Bubble Bars from a cart.

"Can't," said the chief.

"What's that, Chief?"

"I *can't!*" yelled the chief. "Every time I try opening the
door or even sliding sideways, the whole *car* starts to slip.
Where's that fire truck?"

Everyone looked around — then they heard honking and
blaring. The town fire truck came skidding around the corner.

Alongside the water geyser, it sloshed to a stop. The
firepersons hopped off and started splashing around. Everyone
else stood there and watched.

Everyone, that is, except for three kids.

. . .

"Hey," said Luis as he sidled up to Yuke.

"Hello," said Yuke, who was a very nice person. Yuke had stopped digging now, to look at the police car, the water geyser and the firepersons all splashing around.

"You know what? You're some digger," Luis said.

Yuke blushed. "I *can* dig," he said.

"He can dang *well* dig, and now we're in some burr-pickin' pickle because of it!" said Bug Luck. "Aw ..."

Bug was about to fling his hat down and stomp on it again. But Luis said, "You know what? There's another place you could dig."

"That's right," agreed Hayley B. "On the beach."

"Aw ... I don't think so," Bug said, shaking his head. "We're in enough ..."

"There's treasure," breathed Hayley B.

Bug perked up. "Treasure?"

"Yes," she whispered. "It's buried there."

Bug looked at Yuke, and Yuke's big shovel. He said, "*Buried* treasure?"

"Yeah," said Speedup. "Come on!"

Bug looked at all the people, watching the police car atop the water geyser.

"Goin' somewhere else might be a good idea, right now," said Bug.

So he and Yuke and the three kids headed up the side road, toward the beach.

CHAPTER 6

THE BEAUTIFUL BEACH

"HURRY UP," SAID SPEEDUP. "They might come looking for you guys!"

"That's right," whispered Hayley B. "There is great danger."

As they walked, Luis told Bug about the legend of the treasure.

Bug said, "In this town?"

"That's what they say," said Luis.

"Gold and everything?"

"Gold doubloons."

"What the hang flang's a doubloon?"

"I don't know," said Luis. "But it's gold."

"Real gold?"

"Old gold."

Bug thought about that. He nodded. "Old gold is good gold," he said.

They walked some more. "Sure is peculiar," Bug said. "We come the wrong way, and we find gold anyhow."

"We didn't find it yet," Luis pointed out.

"Oh yeah," said Bug. "Dang."

"Can I dig now?" asked Yuke.

"Not yet!" said Hayley B. "Not here."

They came to where the road ends, and the houses end, too. There's a sandy path over low dunes, and then ... the beautiful town beach.

Hayley B. strode ahead. The rest came up. They all stood and looked at that soft, white sand.

The whole town (except for Chief Gherkin) loved this beach. Coming here was the most fun thing to do in Sandy Feet, Florida. In fact, people came from far and wide to relax and have fun on this lovely beach and its soft, white sand.

Beside the beach was a parking lot, for all the people's cars. Because this was a cloudy day, the parking lot was empty. So was the beach.

"You can dig *here*," said Hayley B., sweeping her arm grandly toward the sand.

27

CHAPTER 7

ANOTHER RISING GEYSER

"WHO'D YOU SAY BURIED THIS TREASURE?" Bug asked.

"Jean Lafitte," said Luis. "The pirate king."

"Tell me about him," Bug said.

"Well, he bragged a lot."

"About what?"

"His treasure! See," Luis said, "he had all these people working for him — stealing cargo and stuff. That's why he was the pirate king. He got really rich, from his guys stealing stuff all along the Gulf of Mexico."

Bug scrunched up his face. "What's the Gulf of Mexico?"

"Why — it's this water," Luis said, waving past the beach. "It goes from here all the way to Mexico."

Bug scratched his head. "Mexico," he said. "So *that's* where we are."

"Um, no — we're in Florida," Luis said to Bug. "It's just

that the Gulf of Mexico ..."

"Never mind about that," Bug said. "What did this guy say about his treasure?"

Meanwhile, Speedup and Yuke had rushed onto the beach.

Yuke liked his new friends and he wanted to make them happy, so he began to dig strongly. Very strongly.

Speedup was right beside him. He said, "Dig it, big guy! *Dig* it!"

"Jean Lafitte bragged that he buried his treasure all along the Gulf coast," Luis said. "He said he buried so much gold, if you found it all you could build this huge bridge. All of gold."

Bug scratched his chin. "Why would you do that?"

"You wouldn't," Luis said. "You just could."

"Well, *I* sure wouldn't," Bug said. "I wouldn't mind finding some o' that gold, though."

Bug and Luis weren't watching Yuke and Speedup dig. They were dreaming.

"A big old treasure chest," Bug said. "*Full* of that gold."

"Yeah," said Luis.

. . .

In town, the ladder truck and the firepersons finally, very carefully, got Chief Gherkin down.

The police car was still up there, teetering atop the water. Everyone's feet were sopping and soaked. Everyone still gawked up at the car.

"Everyone get *away* from there," yelled the chief. "Before it slips off!"

The whole town squished wetly, backing up.

Chief Gherkin looked around.

"Hey," he said. "Where'd those weirdos go?"

The whole town looked around.

"Which weirdos, Chief?" said the guy who sold Ice Cream Bubble Bars.

"The weirdos that *did* this, for gosh sake," said the chief. "There was a little noisy one and a big diggin' one. Where'd they *go*?"

The whole town started looking. They looked up one street. They looked down another street. They looked up and down the railroad tracks.

Then somebody said, "Hey — look up the beach road!"

Up that way they could see a high, rising geyser. This time, it was a geyser of sand.

"That's him!" yelled the chief. "That's them! Let's go!"

So on soaking-wet sneakers and sandals and shoes, the whole town squished and squashed and crowded up the road to the beach.

31

CHAPTER 8

PART OF THE OCEAN

WITH HER EYES CLOSED, Hayley B. glided along the edge of the dunes. She was waiting for her intuition to tell her something. Intuition was *very* mysterious.

Hayley B. sniffed. She waited some more.

Then she heard a sound.

Yes! It was a sort of squishing sound. It seemed to be coming this way.

Ah hah, thought Hayley B. — maybe *this* was intuition. She listened closely, waiting and hoping it might tell her where the treasure was.

Well, it wasn't down here. With Speedup beside him saying, "Dig it, big guy! *Dig* it!", Yuke Johnson had done the strongest, fastest, deepest digging of his life. He had dug up that whole beach. The whole thing. It was nothing *but* a hole, now — a very big crater between the sand dunes and the Gulf of Mexico.

And they hadn't found anything. It was nothing but a hole.

Now Speedup heard a rumble. He looked up. The side of the crater closest to the water was washing down. The Gulf of Mexico was coming in.

"Whoa!" Speedup yanked on Yuke's sleeve. "We got to go!"

"'Scuse me?" said Yuke, who was always polite.

"We got to go *now*!"

Yuke looked up to see the wall of the crater collapse. "Uh oh," he said. Grabbing Speedup, he heaved the boy and his shovel up and out of the big hole, onto the sand.

Then Yuke scrambled up himself — just in time.

. . .

"A *million* doubloons?" Bug said, "You think that many?"

"Well," said Luis. "I don't think they were very big."

Running up, Speedup yanked on Luis's t-shirt. "Quick!" he said. "*Look!*"

Luis and Bug finally looked. Where the beach used to be, they saw a huge hole full of water.

"Holy moley," said Luis. "There's no more beach!"

And that was so. The whole nice swimming beach of Sandy Feet, Florida — the *whole* beach, right back to the dunes and all the way down to the parking lot — was gone.

It was just ... gone.

It was part of the Gulf of Mexico now.

Just then, Hayley B. opened her eyes and saw what the squishing sound was. The whole town had come squashing and crowding up the path.

Hayley B. turned toward the beach, to tell her friends they were coming. Then she saw that there was no beach.

"Oh my," she whispered.

Luis, Speedup, Yuke and Bug stood looking at the water.

"Aw, hang flang it," Bug said softly. "Now we're *really* in trouble."

Hayley B. hurried up. "Um," she said. "They're ... well ..."

Bug said, "What?"

She pointed backward, at all the people.

"They're here."

CHAPTER 9
YUKE FEELS BAD

YUKE FELT BAD. He looked at the people as they stared at what used to be their beach. Their beautiful beach. All gone.

They all stood there staring, like they just couldn't believe it.

Yuke knew what he had done. He didn't *mean* to. He only meant to dig up the treasure and make his friends happy.

He looked at good old Bug, and his new friends too. They stood there like statues. They didn't look back.

So Yuke picked up his shovel and just walked away. He walked over to the parking lot, where nobody was looking. Where he could be by himself.

Yuke felt *very* bad. And because he didn't know what else to do, he did the one thing he could do. He did the thing he loved to do. He did the thing that he did.

He started ... to dig.

In fact, because he felt *so* bad, Yuke started digging faster, stronger and deeper than he had ever dug before.

And that is saying something.

CHAPTER 10

PIECES OF PARKING LOT

AT FIRST, AS THEY STARED at what used to be their beach, the whole town was so thunderstruck that nobody could speak. Then everyone started yelling at once.

"How could this happen?" they yelled at each other.

"*How* could this *HAPPEN*?" they yelled at the chief.

The chief yelled back. "I was on top of the water, for gosh sakes!" He pointed to the three kids and Bug Luck. "It's them that did it!"

People hollered, "It's *them*!"

"*They* did this!"

"*They* did?"

"How'd *they* do it, Chief?"

The chief looked around.

"It's the big diggin' one!" he hollered. "Where — hey, *where's the big diggin' one?*"

The whole town looked around — and then, past the three kids and Bug Luck, over by the parking lot they saw a *new* rising geyser. This time it was dirt and sand and chunks of parking lot, all spouting up high in the air.

"Oh no," the chief groaned.

"Oh *no,*" said Speedup — and he took off running for the parking lot. Never mind the falling stuff — he was waving his arms and yelling, as loud as he could: "Hey mister! Hey diggin' man! Hey *stop!*"

Then an angry roar went up from the crowd. The whole town started running, squishing and squashing to get to what used to be the parking lot. To get to Yuke.

Chief Gherkin knew Yuke was big. He knew Yuke was strong. He knew Yuke *had* to be stopped.

He just didn't know how.

Then he heard — then the whole town heard — then Luis, Hayley B. and Bug Luck heard: the thunk.

That's how it sounded, hollow and woodenlike:
THUNK!

CHAPTER 11

THE INCREDIBLE THING

WHEN LUIS, HAYLEY B. and Bug Luck got there — when everyone got there — they all skidded to a stop beside Speedup, at the edge of what used to be the parking lot.

This new crater was not as big, because the parking lot was hard to dig through. But this crater was deeper. Definitely deeper. It was *deep*.

And at the bottom was Yuke Johnson. He was digging, very carefully now, around the edges of the most incredible thing that anyone in Sandy Feet, Florida had ever seen in their lives.

CHAPTER 12

THE MOSQUITO FLEET

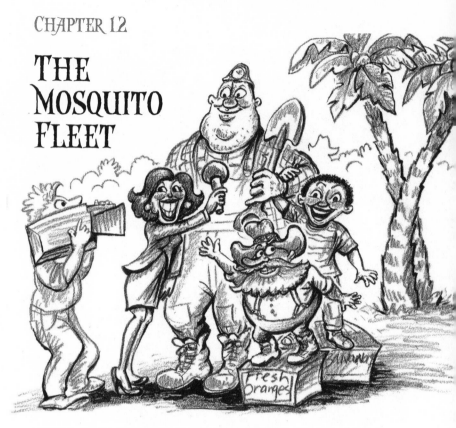

ABOUT TWO HOURS LATER, the TV newslady asked the five heroes, "How did you do it? How did you *find* it?"

"We were looking for doubloons," said Luis.

"It was the sand-flanginest thing," said Bug.

"It was intuition," said Hayley B. "It's very mysterious."

"It was the big guy!" said Speedup. "*He* did it!"

"Did you really?" the newslady asked Yuke. "How?"

Yuke blushed. He was always modest.

He said, "I just ... dug."

It turned out that what Yuke dug up wasn't a pirate ship at all.

It was a pirate hunter.

"This was a ten-gun schooner of the United States Navy," said the man from the Florida Museum of Pirates and Old Ships and Stuff. "That was a type of fast and tough sailing ship. The Navy used it to hunt pirates a long, long time ago.

"Back then, there were pirates all over the Gulf Coast," the man explained. "To find them and stop them stealing cargo and money from innocent ships, the Navy sent a group of fighting vessels down here. People took to calling these ships the Mosquito Fleet.

"For years, those Navy ships chased after the pirates," he said. "Some they captured! But a lot got away."

"Did they chase after Jean Lafitte?" asked Luis.

"Oh yes — and they captured him twice. But he got away both times," the man said. "Then one day in 1823, right around here, there was an awful storm. One of the Navy's pirate-hunter ships just ... disappeared. No one ever knew what happened."

"What do *you* think happened?" asked Hayley B.

"Well, the ship must have wrecked and sunk close to shore," the man said. "Then over time, it got swallowed up in sand. I think the beach slowly built out, and up, right on top of it."

Everyone thought that was pretty amazing. But Luis had another question.

"Did Jean Lafitte ever bury treasure?" he asked. "Like ... maybe ... around here?"

"Well, there are legends about that," said the man from the museum. "Nobody has ever found much treasure, but ... I guess it's always possible."

"I *know* it's true," said Hayley B. "I can feel it!"

43

CHAPTER 13

FUN, FOOD AND HISTORY

WELL, AFTER THAT, things got complicated.
Just about every grownup in Sandy Feet suddenly
thought the unsunken ship might make them a
whole lot of money.

The ship had no treasure, it's true. But people started
talking about how having an unsunken old ship could make
the town famous. If the town *was* famous, they said, then a
whole lot more people would come to Sandy Feet. And they
would spend *lots* of money.

They'd look at the ship — and then they'd buy souvenirs,
and t-shirts, and baseball hats, and postcards, and ice cream
and hot fudge and hot dogs and french fries and chicken
fingers and Ice Cream Bubble Bars. They'd buy peanut butter

fudge and fruit smoothies and shaved ice and
milk shakes and saltwater taffy.

They'd buy coloring books and waffles!
Windup toys and beach toys! Beach shovels
and beach towels! Beach blankets and beach
buckets!

And beach umbrellas!

It was a shining vision. In fact, everyone got
so busy making plans to get rich that they forgot
all about Yuke and Bug and the kids, who after
all had found the boat in the first place.

People were saying they would rebuild the beach. They'd
build a *bigger* beach.

Maybe they'd also build an amusement park with a ferris
wheel and a roller coaster, and bumper cars and a really big
sign saying, "Welcome to Sandy Feet, Home of Fun, Food and
History!"

"Hey," shouted Bug, and he waved his arms. "Hey!"

The whole town turned around.

"Let me tell ya *my* idea," Bug said.

CHAPTER 14

TWO TICKETS TO ALASKA

They came.
They dug

BUG WONDERED if maybe the town should put up a statue of them. The five of them. It was them, after all, that got Sandy Feet on the news shows, and in the newspapers, and made the town pretty famous.

"Don't even *think* about it," said Chief Gherkin — who had not arrested them, after all, which he thought was really pretty nice of him.

The chief shuddered, just to think of a statue like that.

"Ugh," he said.

Then somebody pointed out that the town did not want any more ... um ... digging incidents. And everyone agreed with *that*.

So the whole town bought Yuke Johnson and Bug Luck two first-class tickets on a real, sit-down passenger train, all the way to Alaska.

Which was, of course, where they meant to go all along.

CHAPTER 15

A Picture of Heroes

THE NEXT DAY Hayley B., Luis and Speedup set off walking with Bug and Yuke to the train station. On the way they stopped at the Pirate Diner, where Betty Jo-Ann and Big Thermal were happy to see the heroes.

There were blueberry muffins all around. No charge.

"My," Betty Jo-Ann whispered to Speedup. "He *is* big."

"And he can dig," Speedup whispered back.

"I heard," she said. And she smiled.

Pretty soon the muffins were nothing but blue bits and crumbs.

"Now scoot, you five," said Betty Jo-Ann. "You don't want to miss that train."

They didn't miss it. The train came into the station, all long and silver-shiny. Right before Yuke and Bug got on, Bug said, "Ah, yeah. Well, I got a little something to say."

They waited. They listened. Bug turned red.

"I just ... well ... I-want-ya-to-keep-somethin'," he said very fast. "So maybe you'd remember us."

He took off his hat. He handed it to Luis.

"Your hat?" said Luis.

"Well, sure. I can get another one in Ay-laska," said Bug. "With all the *gold* we'll dig." He winked at Luis.

"You go dig up that whole state," said Luis.

"That's right," said Bug. "How big can Ay-laska be?"

Luis actually knew how big Alaska is. But he just smiled. He didn't want to confuse Bug's big dream.

"Uh ... here," said Yuke, who was always generous. He handed his shovel to Speedup.

Speedup held it. He looked at it.

"You *mean* it?" he said.

"Why, sure," said Yuke. "I can get another one. Besides, it got a little beat up."

But it wasn't beat up to Speedup. It was just about the coolest, toughest thing anyone had ever given him in his life. And the truth is, no one had given him much.

"Whoa," he said, very slowly. "*Whooooa.*"

They all looked at Hayley B.

"Oh," she said. "You don't have to give me anything."

"Well," said Bug, nodding at Yuke. "There *is* one more thing."

And from his overall pocket, Yuke pulled a picture. It was glued on a piece of driftwood.

"It's from one of them newspapers," said Bug.

"We got a glue stick at the store," Yuke added, proudly.

The picture was great. It was the five of them, together the day they dug up Sandy Feet, Florida, and made history. Or found history.

CHAPTER 16

THE TRAIN GOES

"ALL *ABOARD!*" cried the train conductor. Yuke and Bug climbed onto the train. Then Bug stuck his head out the window.

"Well, blangin' flang it," he said to the kids. "Kinda sorry to go after all."

"Yeah," said Luis.

"But we *have* to find that gold," Bug said. "So that's that."

He was gone from the window.

But now Yuke stuck out his head.

"Wish we coulda found that treasure," he said to the kids.

Speedup looked
at his shovel.

"We could still try," he
said.

Hayley B. closed her eyes. "It's
somewhere in Sandy Feet," she said. "I *know* it."

Luis said, "How do you know?"

Her eyes opened wide. "I just ... *do*."

Yuke and Speedup looked at each other. "Do it," said
Speedup. "*Do* it!"

Yuke disappeared into the train. The kids heard Bug say, "Hey! Hey, blingin' fling it — put me *down!*"

Just as the train started moving, Yuke was at the door of the car. Under his arm he had a hairy, noisy, struggling Bug.

"Hey, you big muscle brain," Bug yelled, "put me *down!*"

But instead Yuke hopped off the train, with Bug under his arm.

"Hey," Bug said — "the train's leavin'! *Hey!*"

Yuke set Bug down. He dusted his buddy off.

"No reason to go all that ways," Yuke said to him kindly, "if there's treasure here."

"That's right," said Luis.

"I *know* it's here," Hayley B. said. "Somewhere."

Bug squinted at them. He watched the silver-shiny train pull away.

"I liked them fancy seats," he said.

"I like it here," said Yuke.

Bug looked at all of them. "Well, wingin' ding it. Guess I do too."

Speedup held up his shovel. "I might need some help carryin' this," he said. "It's pretty big."

So Yuke and Speedup held onto that shovel together. They set off walking, back toward town.

Hayley B. and Luis started after them. Bug Luck watched them go.

Then he said, "Hey! Hey, dingin' bing it — wait up!"

THE TRUE STORY ...
I MEAN IT REALLY IS! ...
ABOUT THE PIRATE KING

BY LUIS

Hey, so after all this I went to the library. I found books and websites about pirates, and I learned a lot more about Jean Lafitte.

He was a real guy! I mean, the treasure really *could* be there somewhere.

Here's what I learned:

First, Jean Lafitte wasn't your basic movie-guy pirate. He was more like a businessman. A *pirate* businessman.

The books do say he was handsome, in a bad-guy kind of way. And he was smart! He spoke French, English, Spanish and Italian. He had good manners, and he was very good at being a criminal mastermind.

Jean Lafitte hired other guys to do what pirates did, which was attack ships and steal their cargo. By the year 1810, Jean and his brother, Pierre, had pirate boats roaming all over the Gulf of Mexico. They were based, at that time, in New Orleans, Louisiana. That city was where they sold their stolen cargo.

Jean and Pierre got *so* rich that they built their own port, on an island below Louisiana in the Gulf, to handle their stolen cargo. They later built another "pirate port" on Galveston Island, Texas.

People called Jean Lafitte the Pirate King. His boats and crews were attacking ships and stealing cargo all over the Gulf and the Caribbean Sea. They often used two ports on the Gulf

Coast of Florida, near today's cities of Tampa and Fort Myers.

I live on the Gulf Coast of Florida. This is where the treasure part of the story gets good!

That's because Jean Lafitte liked to brag. His pirates stole millions of dollars, in gold and jewels and stuff — and Jean bragged that they buried this treasure in secret places all over the Gulf coast.

He said he hid so much treasure that if you put it all together, you could build a bridge of gold all the way across the Mississippi River.

Do you know how *wide* the Mississippi River is? Whoa.

But I don't need a gold bridge. I just like to imagine an old wood chest, full of gold coins and stolen jewels, buried somewhere here in Sandy Feet.

What happened to Jean Lafitte? Well, let's face it, he was a big criminal. So after a while, the U.S. Navy sent the "Mosquito Fleet" of fast warships down to the Gulf to get him.

In 1821, they captured Jean Lafitte — but he escaped. They caught him again. He got away again! And the Mosquito Fleet never caught him again.

Then in 1823, off the coast of Cuba, Lafitte tried to raid two Spanish ships. He thought they were full of cargo, but it was a trick — they were really warships in disguise. The Spanish guys turned around and fired their hidden cannons. Jean Lafitte was badly wounded. He died the next day.

And nobody has ever found his treasure. That means it might still be out there!

Somewhere.

THE ALSO TRUE STORY, ABOUT THE GIRL PIRATES WHO WERE BRAVER THAN THE BOYS

BY HAYLEY B.

EXCUSE ME! A lot of people think the pirates were all boys — dirty, cruel, hard-fighting guys.

Oh no! There were dirty, cruel, hard-fighting *girl* pirates too.

I would like to tell their story.

About a hundred years before Jean Lafitte, there was a famous pirate called Calico Jack. "Calico" was a kind of colorful cotton, and Jack loved to wear it. He was known for his style. He was also the pirate who invented the famous skull-and-crossbones flag.

And he fell in love.

Jack was resting on a Caribbean island, taking a vacation from pirating, when he met a beautiful, red-haired girl named Anne Bonny. She was rich, and she had a bad temper.

She was already married to another pirate. But when she met Calico Jack, they both fell in love. So one night they stole a ship from the island harbor, and sailed away.

This is true!

And here's how Anne and Jack spent their honeymoon:
They attacked ships, off the coast of Cuba, and stole their
cargo. (Like Luis said, that's what pirates did.)

Jack and Anne got into a battle with a Spanish warship,
and their boat was badly damaged. Along the Gulf coast of
Florida, where I live, they found a hiding place on a little
island. You can actually visit that island today. Know what it's
called?

Lover's Key. Isn't that great?

After they fixed their ship, Anne and Jack went back to pirating. One day they attacked a boat from Holland, and captured its sailors.

Then Anne noticed something about one of those sailors. He was handsome. He was young ... and he wasn't a boy at all.

He was a girl pretending to be a boy. See, girls weren't supposed to be sailors, back then.

That was very unfair.

So Anne told Calico Jack about the girl, whose name was Mary Read. They all became pirates together — and Anne and Mary grew famous for their bravery.

No one knows what happened to Anne Bonny after she got away from jail. How did she look, how did she dress? Maybe like this?

Whenever the pirates would attack a new ship, those two women were the first to jump aboard, fiercely swinging their swords. They were said to be braver than the guy pirates.

Then one day, in a battle in the dark of night, Calico Jack, Anne Bonny and Mary Read were captured.

On the island of Jamaica, a judge sentenced Calico Jack to be hanged for his crimes. He put the two women in prison.

Mary Read died of a fever, in that island jail — but Anne Bonny got away. Nobody really knows how! It's *very* mysterious.

Some say she went back to pirating, and never got caught again.

That's what I think happened.

And that's the story of the girl pirates who were braver than the guys.

It's *very* true.

OUR THANKS

To raise the funds that we needed to publish *Treasure Town,* we started a campaign on Kickstarter.com. We didn't know if anyone would support our project — but what happened was amazing! Over 130 people, couples and families became Kickstarter backers of this book. We are just so grateful to all the wonderful people who stepped up to help us in this way.

So thank you, Yiota Ahladas and Joni AvRutick, Christine Albrecht, Mary Stokes Anderson, Bonnie Atwater, Elaine Beal, Lindsay Berdan with Kate Ann Feile and Vivi Feile; Julie, Bob, Shannon and Kate Bebee; Bryce Bederka, the Bensons, Ilise Benun, Myra Bleill, Al Boright, Deb Bouton, Dan Bragg, David and Marcia Bragg, Eric Bragg, Robert and Polly Bragg, the Trish and Tully Bragg family, Bob Brannan and Rosalind Osterbye, Tim, Anne, Eliana, and Maclyn Buckingham; Marialisa Calta, the Campbell Family, Becky Carlson, Jack Carter, Bill Cater; Ray, Shannon, Melissa and everyone at *Choose Your Own Adventure*; Kokona Chrisos-Tsataros, Liz Cleveland, David Cohen, Nina Coombs, Jen, Julie and James Cotignola, Colette Crescas, Britt and Michele Cummings, Dana Cummings and Kristin Bair-Cummings, Diane and Gabrielle Cummings and Ted Coles, and Mark, Debbie, Heather and Danielle Cummings.

Also Pam Dean, Janet DiBlasi, Cathie Dinsmore, Mark Domeier, Tom and Martha Douglass, Wendi Dowst-McNaughton, Geoff and Sally V. Dugan, Barbara and Jack Dugan, Sally E. Dugan, Derek Duff, Lynn Fanella, Brandon and Charlie Farrow, Suzanne and Chuck Flynn, Evelyn M. Foley, Sarah Forbes, Betsy Fram, Stephen Frey and Arocordis Design, Kitty Friedman, Tom Garrett-Kraus, Beth Gilpin and Mark Powell, Linda Gilpin, Eileen Gilshian, Ramona Godfrey, David Goodman and Sue Minter, Gary and Karen Grange, Jerry Greenfield, George Hamilton, Kaiser and Kira Hart, Pat Hazouri and Chris Owen, Molly Henick, John Himmel and Kim Kubiak, Kathryn Grill Hoeppel, Wendy James, Charles Kletecka, Mark Kolter, Carolyn Goodwin Kueffner, Bonnie

Our friend Brent Campbell was one of our top Kickstarter backers. Brent's dad, David Campbell, loved to race cars and to watch auto racing. His race cars all had "E3" as their number.

Insull and Richard Scher, Lori Johnston and Venus Corriveau, Karen Kantor, Barbara and Richard Kurz, Ahnna Lake, Fritz Laporte, Izaiah Trae Lesher, Anne and John Lika, David and Margaret Luce, and Trudy Ludwig.

Also Bill Maclay, Maureen Martin, Bob and Cindy Maynard, Sharon McCrae, Monica McEnerny, Jim Mendell, the Mickleys, Ellen Miles, Annabelle and Maxwell Miller, Gordon Miller, Mary and Sam Miller, Dawn, Bill and Sophia Minter, M.K. Monley and Don Schneider, Tim and Sharon Newcomb, Jan Novack, Donna O'Malley and David Allen, the Patterson Family, Andy, Bryn, Skyler and Haley Perkins, Andrea Perrin, Julie Pickett, Geoff Poister, Robert Resnik and Maureen Cannon; Kristin Richland, Magda, Simone, Penny and Jonah Riha; Dillon Riley, Nancy Rote, Ryan, Catie, Jake and Sam Ruggiero; the Sanford Readers, Hank and Ruthie Santini, Lisa Scagliotti and William Brundage, Ted Schelvan, Ted Scheu, Liz Schlegel and Tom Stevens, Lyn Severance and Bill Harvey, Carolyn Shapiro, Nichole Simmons, Gerianne Smart, Mike Snapke, Kurt, Heather and Colin Snyder, Janet Spaulding, Anne Bragg Stedman and family, Mike, Emily, and Ryan Stephens, Carol Stenberg, Sally Stetson, Edgar Stewart, Jim and Liz Stokes, Kayne Strippe, Maggie Symington,

John and Denny Tibbets, Ilona Engel Travis, Anita Warren, Bradley
Wilhelm, Chris Wilhelm, Gordon Wilhelm, the Woods Family, Lois Hottell
Wood and Patty Worsham.

For help with this project, we would also like to thank the administration,
staff and students at the Mary Hogan Elementary School in Middlebury,
Vermont, especially school librarian Julie Altemose. And we're grateful to
Sue Biggam, Scottie Brower, Marianne Doe, Grace Butler, Lynn Gatto,
Steve Kasdin, Ellen Miles, Ray Montgomery, Sarah Stewart Taylor and
Cris Jones of Factotum.

Lastly, but also kind of firstly, we thank our spouses, Heath Cummings
and Cary Beckwith, for their great support and encouragement, and
Tim Newcomb of Newcomb Studios in Montpelier, Vermont, for designing
this book in such a fun and beautiful way.

Doug and Sarah-Lee